S0-ARL-774

Now the party is over. It is time to leave. The birthday boy waves good-bye to his guests.

"What a nice birthday party it was," he says.

"M-m-m-m-m, the cake is so good and the ice cream is yummy," say the guests.

Everyone gathers around the table and sings "Happy Birthday." The birthday boy makes a wish and blows out the candles.

It is time to open the presents. The birthday boy gets a harmonica, a book, a paint set, and a toy drum.

"Thank you," he says. "I like all my presents."

The littlest Monchhichi wins.

There is a prize for dropping
the most clothespins in a bottle.

Mommy plays the piano for a game of Musical Chairs.

The Monchhichi friends play Pin the Tail on the Donkey.

“Happy birthday,” they say.

They do come. The Monchhichi boys and girls are all dressed up and carrying presents.

The birthday boy waits
for the guests to arrive.
"Will they come?" he says.

Daddy hangs streamers, the birthday boy puts party hats on the table, and Mommy blows up balloons. Everything is ready.

Mommy is making a very special cake for the birthday party.

Today is a very special day for the Monchhichi birthday boy. He is having a party. He puts on his party clothes to look his best.

The Original Monchhichi™

Happy Birthday

by Sally Trimble
illustrated by Manny Campana

A GOLDEN BOOK • NEW YORK
Western Publishing Company, Inc., Racine, Wisconsin 53404

 ISBN 0-307-12246-8 A B C D E F G H I J